SANREVELLE

McSWEENEY'S
SAN FRANCISCO

Copyright © 2025 Dave Eggers

This is the seventh in a series of stories that will, god willing, someday become something larger, called *The Forgetters*.

This story, in slightly different form, was first published in *The Georgia Review*, and also the 2025 O. Henry Prize collection.

All rights reserved, including right of reproduction in whole or in part, in any form. McSweeney's and colophon are registered trademarks of McSweeney's, an independent, nonprofit publishing company based in San Francisco.

Cover illustration by Annie Dills.

ISBN: 978-1-963270-41-9

These numbers could mean anything, or nothing:
10 9 8 7 6 5 4 3 2 1

www.mcsweeneys.net

Printed in Canada

SANREVELLE

by

DAVE EGGERS

McSWEENEY'S

For Captain H.

SANREVELLE SAID she would be at her boat, but she was not at her boat and the sky was darkening fast. The Procession of Illuminated Vessels had no set start time, so you had to be ready. Once the sky was black it began, and in December the dark could come at half past five.

Hop stood on the dock beside Sanrevelle's boat, a thirty-two-foot schooner called the *Cradle*, and saw no sign of her. There were no lights on in the cabin. He called her phone and got no answer. She'd said if she wasn't at the *Cradle* she'd be at the Waterfront Social Club, so he walked down her rickety dock, back to the rocky shore, past the ramshackle community garden and over to the Club. He had to think of a way to get past Walter, the bouncer, who'd done twenty-two years at Vacaville for armed robbery and checked Social Club membership cards at the door.

That the Waterfront Social Club had a bouncer at all was an act of great hubris, given that the Club was no more than a decommissioned barge sitting on the mud between the bay and the town. The interior of the barge looked like a seventies rec room. The floors were sticky, the beer, served in cloudy plastic cups, cost three dollars, and the food was warmed in a microwave by Walter's nineteen-year-old daughter. At high tide the barge briefly rose from the mud for an hour or two before settling again into the muck, which was gray and smelled strongly of fish, eelgrass, engine oil and gasoline.

When Hop reached the door, Walter was not perched on his stool as usual, so Hop quickly slipped into the Club unseen. He ducked past the big-screen television and around the lacquered tables, past the bookshelf filled with mid-century board games and 1870s sextants, and out to the back deck that faced the bay. A few dozen drinkers were gathered there, squinting into the night, waiting for the lighted boats to assemble and pass by like waterborne Christmas trees.

The parade had been going on since before electricity. Around 1880, a Norwegian seaman had decked his ketch out in candles and Chinese lanterns and had sailed around the town at night to celebrate the birth of Christ. His sail had caught fire and he'd almost died, but the tradition had carried on, and when not hampered by fog or war or local political rivalries, the parade produced otherworldly beauty for a few hundred shorebound spectators. Boaters decorated their sails, outlined their hulls in lights, bought inflatable snowmen and Santas; every year one tugboat carried fifty children, dressed as Mary and Joseph and sheep, all of them ghostly white against the dark, dark water.

Hop wove through the revelers in the Club, many of whom had brought their own beer to avoid the three-dollar charge. He didn't see Sanrevelle, didn't see any of her crowd. The parade watchers were a mix of aging hippies, salty and single, and the newer Club members, decades younger, with their very young children, who were crouching at the edge of the barge, using mussel meat tied to string to try to catch crabs amassed near the hull.

Then Hop saw Sanrevelle's skeptical friend Joy. She was drinking gin through a figure-8 straw. Her eyes opened wide as she finished a long pull. "You just missed her," she said, and nodded toward the water. "Gwen came by on her skiff and Sanrevelle went with."

"Oh," Hop said, and looked out to the gathering of lighted boats in the distance, arranging themselves into linear form. From where he stood, the boats were like neon toys tossed into deepest space. He tried not to appear forlorn, but he was sure this was how he looked—like a desperate man of thirty-eight, arriving alone to a bar, looking for a woman out there, somewhere in the velvet black.

Hop worked as a paralegal for a personal-injury law firm, and the firm was collapsing as its founder lost his mind. Hop walked in one day to find this sixty-four-year-old man, Sam Whistler, partner of Whistler and Wong, on Zoom, talking with a Turco-French psychic in Bordeaux. "That is exactly what happened," Whistler said to his psychic, voice awed. Hop had come to get clarity on an enigmatic invoice, but left his boss to his internet prophet. Later, Whistler came to Hop's desk. "That guy knew things about me that he simply could not know. When I'm done I want you to see him, too. He'll change your life."

Whistler began teleconferencing with the Bordeaux shaman daily. After a few weeks of readings, one morning he thrust a small toiletry bag into Hop's hand. "Take these away from me," Whistler said. Inside there was a business-style envelope full of psychedelic mushrooms. "That's about five thousand dollars there," he said. "I would have flushed them, but I thought you might want them, or know someone who would." He looked out the window, then down at the street far below. "And if my brother calls, tell him I'm out. He has cancer and I can't get involved."

The firm's offices were on the fortieth floor of the Millennium Tower, built on clay and sinking two or three inches every year. The engineers were baffled, the geologists amused, and the owners of the building were obliged to reduce the rent. Whistler had asked Hop to take over paying that and most other bills; he didn't trust Cecilia, his right hand, anymore. His medium in Bordeaux had a bad feeling about Cecilia, starting with her name—the letters, translated to numbers, added up to an unlucky sum.

The firm kept the lights on, but Whistler, far and away its most important earner, came and went at odd hours, and had stopped taking on new work. Soon the part-time help was laid off. Résumés were updated and attorneys fled. Whistler proposed dance parties and was visited by an eclectic parade of women of all ages with dangerously long fingernails. They arrived for lunch appointments in Whistler's office and he stumbled out afterward, struggling not to slur.

One day Whistler insisted that he and Hop become better friends. He'd read an article that said men needed friendships in middle age, so he brought Hop to a Giants game, and talked for three hours about his mother. He said he was working on himself. He said he was finding his own true north. He said he was microdosing and that most of the people in his life were toxic and manipulative. He asked not one question about Hop and stood up in the seventh inning, saying he needed to use the bathroom. He never returned.

"Hop, you're the glue that holds this place together," he confided a week later. The next day he said the same thing to his secretary, Janet, and then to Philip, the building's chief engineer, whose staff was unionizing. Soon they were on strike, and Philip had left for Cabo San Lucas. Only one of the eight elevators worked, and even then sporadically. The heat went off and on. There was no air-conditioning. The building was usually dark, half-abandoned, and began to smell of hidden decay. The remaining staff of Whistler and Wong, most of them working from home, began to quit. Janet moved to British Columbia to become a wildlife photographer. No one saw the point in what they were doing in the Millennium, and Whistler didn't seem to, either.

But someone had to stand guard over the remnants of the firm. "Will you live here?" Whistler asked Hop. "There are no guards in the lobby and the electronic locks don't work. I have to leave the doors open or else I'll never get back in. Can you move in? I'll get you a bed. Sublet your place. Make a profit."

Hop moved into the tower but kept his apartment. He thought it would be a week, maybe two. But after six months Whistler had become even more elusive and vague, and Hop left his apartment and its $3,400 monthly rent. He lived for free on the Millennium's fortieth floor and had most of it to himself, his bed in a former conference room, a vast kitchen, long carpeted hallways he traversed on Whistler's pristine mountain bike; Hop had been given this, too. When the phone rang, usually Hop let it ring, but occasionally, for a lark, he picked up.

"Does anyone work there anymore?" the caller invariably asked.

"No," Hop would say cryptically. "I am alone in the tower."

During the day he pressed his forehead to the floor-to-ceiling glass and looked out at the vast blue bay, wanting to be there, on some boat, and not here, in a sinking building whose windows didn't open. He would spot some tiny sailboat, just a bright white shard against the sea of hammered blue, and would picture himself on it, sea spray in his face, roaring through whitecaps, yelling greetings and admonitions to fellow sailors, heading through the Golden Gate and into the madness of the Pacific.

* * *

One Sunday he found himself in a ramshackle marina in a brightly colored little town, waiting in his car for a sailing instructor. He'd been told to arrive at 9 a.m. but at 9 a.m. he saw only a raggedy-haired woman wearing mismatched layers, wools and plaids, struggling with a locked gate. He thought she might be trying to break into the place.

Finally she looked up and at him. Her face opened into a wide smile and she crossed the parking lot in a few long strides and was suddenly at his window.

"Hop? Are you Hop?"

He rolled down his window.

"I'm Sanrevelle," she said. "You ready? You're still in your car."

He'd expected an older, sunburned country-club gentleman, but Sanrevelle was frizzy, sturdily built, a few years older than him. Her skin was olive-colored and taut and her hair was a swirling black mass. He half expected her to pull things from the thicket— pencils or maps or food.

"I'm thinking we just go out and learn as we go," she said, and led him around the gate she'd been trying to open, down a battered gray dock and to a catamaran, its flat surface no bigger than a child's trampoline. She fitted him for a life preserver. There were no safety talks, no questions, no instructions.

"Sit there," she said, and he scooted from the dock and onto the catamaran. She stepped onto the other side, sat down and took the line of the sail—he didn't know the right term and she didn't tell him— and they were off. In seconds they sped a hundred yards into the bay. "Can you swim?" she asked. They were pointed toward Alcatraz. He said he could, and he squinted into the sunlight on the water, the way it moved like a flashlight zigzagging in the dark. He was momentarily hypnotized, taken out of time. He lived in that golden flickering for a while, and found himself closing his eyes, feeling the shimmer on his face, his eyelids. They'd been sailing for ten minutes and he was already changed by these colors, this abandon. There were no lanes on the bay, nowhere to be or not to be. They were shooting diagonally into a manic light.

"Hold on," Sanrevelle said, and tacked to get out of the way of a thunderous yellow-and-black ferry loaded with tourists, and when it had passed and they crossed its wake, Hop got soaked, the water icy and seizing every part of him—hands, feet, bones.

"Gusts over there," she said. She spoke this way, in fragments, leaving out words. "Porpoises," she said a few minutes later, and Hop saw two of them, their curved dorsal fins riding a swift current west. When he turned back to Sanrevelle, she was looking at his footwear.

For the lesson, Hop had bought, online, a kind of sneaker that had separate homes for each toe. He thought they might help him avoid falling off wet and slippery boat decks.

"I've seen pictures of those, but never in person," Sanrevelle said. "Are they comfortable?" Her tone was half-amused, half-aghast.

"They feel very strange," he admitted. "Almost lewd."

She laughed. "You don't need gear to sail."

"Okay," he said.

"Like you don't need tight shorts to ride a bike."

"I know."

"Take them off then," she said, and removed her own shoes. She tied her sneakers, canvas and torn, together and to the mast. Hop took off his shoes, too, and tied them to the mast, too, making an awkward mound of footwear around the clean aluminum pole. The trampoline surface of the catamaran felt good under his bare feet, like the skin of a snake.

"Indoor feet," she said about Hop's. Hers were calloused and blistered, and she was missing two toenails.

"I take it you work in the city?" she asked.

He pointed to the Millennium Tower and explained that he worked there and lived there, too.

"The one that's sinking?" she asked. "You have an escape plan?"

Hop told her about Whistler, how he'd lost his mind, and how the building staff had quit, and how Hop dreamed most nights that the tower was collapsing. In this dream, his face was pressed to the glass as the building fell toward Market Street. He could only watch as the pavement swung up to smash him.

"And then you wake up," she said.

"And then I wake up," he said.

"You could move," Sanrevelle said, and a gurgling sound caught her attention. "Look," she said, and nodded to a polished black orb that had just emerged from the bay. "That's probably Sarah." Sarah was a seal and the orb was her head. She followed them for few hundred yards before disappearing into the reflection of the sun. They tacked awhile near Alcatraz, the waves rolling under them with growing power and menace.

"So is Hop short for something?" Sanrevelle asked.

"Family last name. Hopland. I think it means that somewhere, at some point, we grew hops."

Sanrevelle had lost interest in the history of his name. "Check it out," she said, and nodded toward a dark blur coming from the southern sky. "Supposed to rain. We'll head in." She turned the catamaran around and they skipped along the surface like a water bug. They got to the dock just as the rain began to come down, a silvery torrent that drenched them as they tied up the boat. He paid her in cash, $120 for two hours, and he asked when they could go again.

"Like a weekend or a weekday?" she asked.

Hop wondered to himself whether Whistler would care if he skipped a day or a month. No, he thought, he probably wouldn't notice. "Any day, anytime," Hop said. "No one cares anymore."

Even after the first lesson, he knew that Sanrevelle was the last capable and sane person in his life. Everyone else was lost, medicated, overwhelmed, drawn endlessly to their past, searching fruitlessly for clues as to why they were who they were, and not someone else. Whistler hadn't been seen at the office in six weeks. The staff was down to seven, all but Hop working from home. There was one practicing attorney, Gilbert Escovedo, who was looking for a new firm and one day brought movers to the building and took away much of the furniture. Hop didn't know if Whistler had approved this or not, and he didn't have the standing to challenge it.

The last time he'd seen Whistler, he was deep in a new therapy, unlicensed and run by a group calling itself the Urgers, that sought to redirect adult lives by finding "microfaults" in the patient's parents. Whistler had prepared a list, four pages long and growing, of the mistakes his parents, dead before the turn of this century, had apparently made; he asked

Hop to make three copies. Hop had glanced at the top of the page, where Whistler had written "Not enough botany." His parents had encouraged him to go to law school, and this, Whistler now surmised, was an act of great evil. Turns out he should have been a sculptor; the internet psychic had uncovered this. Had it not been for his parents, he was certain, he would have been Rodin. Whistler was sixty-four years old and had become a grievance-based adolescent, casting about for complaints against the defenseless dead.

But Sanrevelle was not confused about herself or her place in the world, and was not at war with her long-gone progenitors. Every day she sailed passengers into the bay, sometimes under the Golden Gate Bridge, then sailed back. She was paid to show people the sea, and every morning she had a plan, to sail and show and keep her passengers from harm. She waved to the Coast Guard. She checked life preservers. She trimmed sails and filled her tank with gas. She battened hatches.

And she wanted to sail to the Sea of Cortez. She hadn't done it yet, but would do it—probably in the new year, maybe even January. She'd been planning it, and needed a crew of two plus herself. She told Hop this on their second lesson, when they shot across the bay to the point of Tiburon and for a while, when the wind died, they just sat, bobbing on the water's silky surface.

"If I knew you better, I'd take you," she said. "You're easy to be around." This was the first time she'd made any assessment of him; it seemed to be the first time she'd noticed him as anything more than a client, a passenger with bad shoes.

"I'd go with you," Hop said, trying to sound casual. "I haven't sailed to the Sea of Cortez, either. I can cook. You need a cook?"

She took off her sunglasses and assessed him. Her eyes were green, bright, hiding under squinty folds. "Maybe," she said finally.

And Hop knew that that's what he needed to live for—to be chosen by Sanrevelle, to sail to the Sea of Cortez as her mate. He knew little about sailing, and nothing about sailing to the Sea of Cortez. Was it dangerous? He pictured hundred-foot waves and orcas, maybe sea dragons. Did people really sail in little boats all the way to the Sea of Cortez? It seemed unnecessary, and long, and likely tedious, all those weeks without land. But he would follow her anywhere.

On their third lesson she took him out on the *Cradle*, and they sailed around Angel Island. The wind was light and westerly, so when they sailed to the eastern side of the island, they were protected and the temperature seemed to double; she dropped anchor. They took her tiny dinghy to the beach and sat together on that empty shore, facing Berkeley and El Cerrito, and she drew up her bare feet, sole to sole, and told him about growing up in Lisbon, at least till she was ten, then finding her way to Maine, then Indiana, then Coral Gables, then finally to California. She'd been married once, to a man who worked in marine construction and lived in Alameda. Hop sat and listened and tried to seem professionally aloof, but he was very much in love already, and then she took off her hoodie.

She wore hoodies always, usually navy blue and bearing her company logo, a signal flag and the words SAIL WITH ME! But that day on the beach was warm, and the wind suddenly died, and then she was taking

17

the sweatshirt off, and while her face was hidden in the cottony folds, he glanced her way and saw her shape, her full breasts and lean muscles and soft belly and a ragged purple scar running from her left elbow to her palm. He looked quickly away, but thought then, and for weeks after, of the fool he'd been as a young man, assuming that anyone in their thirties or forties was wrinkled and saggy, when the miracle of it was that he was thirty-eight and hadn't changed much at all, and Sanrevelle's own shape was surely more interesting now than it had ever been—bursting with contradictions, soft and hard and fleshy and full of intrigue and power.

"Should we swim or would that be crazy?" she asked. It was the first time she'd expressed any doubt about anything.

They waded into the cold, cold bay, and stayed in the shallows, swimming and diving. Her nest of black hair was briefly wet, shrinking like wool, but seemed to dry in seconds. Her T-shirt clung to her, a dark-colored bra beneath. She pulled at her shirt to separate it from her soaked skin, and then excused herself to walk up to where the beach met the trees.

"Gonna wring this out," she said, and he stared at the water, and glanced at the Bay Bridge, where cars, just glistening dots, moved sluggishly into the city. When he looked back, she'd put her hoodie back on and was dragging the dinghy back to the water.

"Yeah, I could never date a middle-aged thumb-sucker," she said. She seemed to be concluding a conversation she'd been having with herself. She dropped the bow of the dinghy into the water and covered her eyes with a stiff hand to look at him. "You're not a middle-aged thumbsucker, are you?"

"No, I'm not a middle-aged thumbsucker," he said.

"You're not working out mommy issues in your forties?"

"I'm not," he said.

"Get in," she said, and with one long sandy stride from Sanrevelle they were afloat. Did this mean she saw him as a romantic prospect? By nature, he was dense about such things. And she was the captain, the teacher. Maybe she was just thinking aloud—something she often did.

"Jump out first," she said.

They'd reached the *Cradle* and soon she was onto other things—the bad weather coming in from the west and the location, somewhere under the sea near Angel Island, of a safe containing $1 million in gold bullion, lost in a shipwreck from 1913. "How hard could it be to find it?" she asked. "The bay is big, but not that big."

Then she was onto the topic of tabernacle masts. She planned to replace one of the *Cradle*'s with a tabernacle mast, she said, once she got to Mexico.

"Cheaper down there," she said, and she could sleep on the beach while the shipwrights worked. The wind picked up just then, and her black hair spread like ink all over the sky. "Let's head back in," she said.

After each lesson he would return to the city, exhausted, sun-soaked, his shoes wet, his skin dry, his hair full of salt, and he would feel braided into the earth and sea. He would feel that this was the only way, so obviously the right way, to live—to spend the days out on the water with Sanrevelle, every spray of the ocean like a baptism. And then he would park on Market Street and walk into the Millennium Tower, would be seized by its sour suffocated smell, its wretched stained carpet, the elevator like a coffin rising to his floor, where he would rush back to the wall of windows and look back to the sea below, wanting to be out there in the fight and flow.

Joy knew his intentions. He was sure of it. She lived on a different boat, a converted pontoon cruiser a few docks away, laden with potted plants, and she called Sanrevelle "Revvy." She saw through Hop, seemed to have gleaned the exact moment when Hop knew he was in love. Hop had been following Sanrevelle down the dock after a lesson, carrying his life vest and backpack, and he must have been staring at Sanrevelle's shape, her sprightly, purposeful walk, her jogging shorts and tanned legs.

"Hi Hop!" Joy had said. She'd come out of nowhere and was quickly between Hop and Sanrevelle, looking at him like she'd caught him at something. "Good lesson, Hop? Enjoying your lessons with Revvy, Hop?" Joy was far younger, maybe just thirty, and looked upon Hop as a sad sack, a city guy hopelessly out of place.

But now, on this night of the Procession of Illuminated Vessels, as Hop was staring out at the distant neon lights, thinking he had no way to get to them, Joy said, "You know..." Then she sipped from her figure-8 straw and closed one eye, as if looking at him through an invisible telescope. "You could go find her. Borrow something. That canoe will get you there."

She pointed to the Waterfront Social Club's lower deck, where a dozen kayaks and canoes and paddle-boards were stacked without care. Members of the Club were allowed to keep them there, provided that they be available for other members to borrow freely. It was a hippie system that worked for everyone but resulted in profound wear and tear to the vessels involved.

"She's probably not far," Joy added, and took another long pull on her straw. "Take the canoe."

Hop walked down the ramp and turned the canoe over. A small creature, a chipmunk or crab, scurried away. Hop dragged the canoe loudly across the deck and into the water, looking for signs of Walter.

"Just take it?" Hop asked.

"Jesus, Hop, yes," Joy said.

Hop set the aluminum canoe into the black water. It bounced like a baby on a bed. He looked for a paddle and found a heavy wooden one, old and splintered, in a nearby rowboat. He crawled into the canoe, wanting to do as Joy had said, to seem confident, and so pushed off with the end of the paddle, realizing too late that he wasn't dressed for the bay in December—he was wearing jeans and sneakers and a canvas jacket—and he hadn't brought a life vest. It was too late to go back, he decided. And yet the canoe was no more than a concavity, a half tube of metal, a noncommittal promise of protection. In it he was dry and safe, but all around was icy water; he'd be hypothermic in minutes.

He left the lights of the Club, the shrieking laughter and muffled sound system growing fainter as he paddled into the dark. He looked toward the scrum of bright lights in the distance, and paddled—two strokes on the left, two on the right. The water was calm, the wind light, but the air couldn't have been more than fifty degrees, and felt colder with each lunge deeper into the bay. The whinny of a small motorboat startled him, and he watched as a single man in a tiny skiff crossed his path, a dog sitting upright on the bow. The boat's wake gave a shimmy to the canoe, and Hop set the paddle across it, steadying himself.

Passing a long dock running parallel to the shore, Hop saw a pair of beach chairs occupied by dolls.

"Where are you going?" a boy's voice asked. They were children, not dolls. They appeared to be about six or seven. He couldn't see the boy's face, only his silhouette. There were no parents in sight.

"This way," Hop said, and pointed with his paddle.

"Are you cold?" the other child, a girl, asked.

"Not yet," Hop said.

"You don't have any lights on your canoe," the girl said. "You're supposed to have lights."

"That's where I'm going, actually," Hop lied. "To get some lights at the light store." He pointed into the bay. "Where are your parents?" he asked.

"There's no light store out there!" the boy said, but Hop had already paddled away. He was headed toward a big red tugboat called the *Excelsior*. Its owner was a friend of Sanrevelle's, and Hop thought there was an outside chance she'd be onboard. Though it was moored to a long dock, and not decorated for the parade, there were figures in the bright windows and he heard voices coming from the deck.

Hop was halfway to the tug when a herd of watery ravers came his way. They were paddleboarders festooned with glowing necklaces and bracelets and hats, their boards outlined in pink and purple LEDs.

"There's a guy in a canoe," a voice said from the dark, and they paddled past him in silence, seeming wary. They were heading south, to the central parade-viewing area in town, and when they were gone, Hop was alone, and he looked into the sky to see a one-quarter moon set within a gauzy ring, a promise of rain tomorrow.

The rumble of a small motor brought his attention to the piers behind him.

"Who's that?" a man asked. The man's voice was parched, reed thin.

"Just me," Hop said, though he realized that his answer would not clarify much.

"Me who?" the man asked, and now Hop could see a hunched figure at the back of an aluminum boat, its outboard no bigger than a vacuum cleaner.

"I don't think you know me," Hop said. "I'm just here for the parade."

"No, no. Your voice sounds familiar," the man said. "What's your name?"

"Peter," Hop lied.

"Peter Pumpkin, or Peter Pan?" the man asked, his voice taking a hard turn.

"Just Peter," Hop said, and paddled in the direction of the tug. "Have a good night."

"Peter Pumpkin or Peter Pan?" the man yelled to Hop's back.

Hop paddled hard for the tug, which seemed to rise higher as he got closer. A gust of wind came down from the headlands and someone from the tug yelled, "Put a weight around it!" Hop looked up to the deck to find two people wrestling with a six-foot penguin, a lawn decoration, lit from within. The two people were attempting to fasten it to the stern of the tugboat. But then the wind gusted again and lifted the penguin into the air and—"No! No!" a woman screamed—it arced downward, slowly and almost gracefully, onto the surface of the bay, where it quickly deflated, went dark, and began to sink.

The two figures leaned over the edge of the tug, laughing hysterically, slashing a beam from their flashlight into the obsidian water. And then they saw Hop.

"You! Save our penguin!"

"Yes, can you?"

They thought this was beyond funny, that the penguin might be rescued by a guy in a canoe. Hop paddled to the plastic mess, and found it stiff and heavier than expected, but easy enough to save, and when he had the penguin safely inside his concavity, the light within it went bright again, as if resurrected.

"He got it! He got it!" the revelers roared from above. "It's a Christmas miracle!" they yelled, and then laughed till they were breathless. By now, there were a half dozen people on the deck of the tug, wanting to witness the rescue. Hop paddled closer to the *Excelsior* and a rope was lowered. He tied it around the waist of the deflated penguin and it was lifted, still lit from within, up to the tug, and once it was aboard, a roar of applause burst out.

"Thank you, Paddle-to-the-Sea," he heard a woman's voice say. "Can you come aboard? Just tie up at the pier and use the gangplank."

Now Hop could see faces, beautiful faces, above, and in the portholes at eye level, everyone fascinated by the man in the canoe who had saved the illuminated bird. Hop wanted to paddle off, like a cowboy would, but then remembered why he'd approached the tug.

"Is Captain Sanrevelle aboard?" he asked.

"Is Captain Sanrevelle aboard?" the woman repeated to the people assembled on the deck. She seemed to know Sanrevelle, and her tone implied there was a real possibility she was there on the tug. For a moment Hop felt sure that Sanrevelle would be there—the tug was owned by her friend, and it was a logical place from which to watch the parade. The penguin-salvation, too, now seemed inevitable—a logical step to his finding her, proving himself while she was close.

The woman returned. "Nope," she said. "Paulie saw her on the shark-yacht, though. You know that one?" She pointed out into the bay, to the tangle of bright vessels struggling to get themselves into parade order. "Come aboard anyway," the woman said. "We have glögg here, and..." She retreated again and emerged holding a bottle of gin. "Locally made!" she said. "You know Scott?"

Hop did not know Scott, but thanked her and said he was moving on.

"Wait!" the woman said, and shone a flashlight on herself. "We're sending you off with a gift." She wrapped the bottle in a beach towel and tied a line around it. She lowered the bundle to him, and because it was too complicated to refuse it, he thanked her, sent the line back to them, and turned the canoe around and pointed himself into the bay, where the procession of lighted boats was newly in a semblance of a line.

"Goodbye, penguin-savior!" a man said, and Hop looked back to see that they'd arranged the penguin upright again, and someone was making the bird wave down to him. Hop raised his paddle to the penguin and the *Excelsior*, and then startled when a loudspeaker burst to life with a deafening scratch.

Hop turned to find an enormous white yacht approaching, bright with a thousand tiny white and pink lights. It looked like a casino unmoored, and the speakers sent a mid-century holiday song into the air.

It was Dean Martin's "Let It Snow!"—brassy and even a bit lewd, a distinctly adult, nightclub version of the song, though none of the words had changed.

Hop had to paddle backward quickly to stay out of the yacht's path. The passengers couldn't see him, would have no chance of seeing him so far below, given that he was so small, without lights and drifting in the shifting shadows. As the boat passed, he saw fifty or so people aboard, wearing antlers and necklaces of alternating lights. The mass of guests on the main deck yelled "Woo!" to no one in particular, while a small group sat still on the bow, all clad in white gowns—ghostly costumes of sleep or the afterlife. Hop assumed they had something planned for the judging stand a half mile south, though for the moment they looked dour and cold. The yacht passed, and its wake tipped Hop's canoe left and right, left and right, and the bottle of gin rocked on the floor, tempting him.

Hop picked it up and took a sip. It was bitter but sugary, too—dangerously easy going down. He took another sip and recapped the bottle.

"Heads up, bro," a man's voice said, just behind Hop. He turned to find an inscrutable pattern of lights approaching. There were two horizontal blue stripes near the water, and above them, a zigzag of fast-moving yellow lights. It was a small craft, just big enough for the one man.

"You know how much further to the reviewing stand?" the man asked, panting hard. By now Hop saw that he was wearing a wetsuit festooned with LEDs, and was pedaling a bicycle mounted on pontoons, each of them strung with lights, too. The contraption was wildly inefficient, a desperate sort of locomotion.

"You're almost there," Hop said, while knowing that at the man's plodding pace it would take him another hour.

"Thanks, bro," the man said. "You good?"

"I'm good," Hop said.

"You don't have any lights," the man said. "Scary for you."

"Just looking for a friend on the shark-boat," Hop said.

"What friend? Clara?"

Feeling he had nothing to lose, and because this man seemed anxious for conversation, Hop said he was looking for Sanrevelle.

"Captain Sanrevelle?" the man asked. "I just saw her twenty minutes ago. She was on Maya's boat. See?"

Hop sensed that the man was pointing, but because his arms weren't lighted, he couldn't know for sure.

"Over there. Little dinghy with the light rings. Near the Christmas trees."

"Was she with Gwen?" Hop asked, and immediately realized that this did not matter.

"I don't think I know Gwen," the man said. By now his continued pedaling and conversation had exhausted all his breath. He was hoarse and heaving.

"Thanks," Hop said, and let him pass.

Beyond the pontoon man, on a promontory jutting into the bay, there was a small operation selling Christmas trees. From the water it looked like a tiny forest, the treeline orderly and lit from above by garlands of white lights. Against their glow, a small boat with two figures aboard was moving out from the rocky beach. Even from a hundred yards away Hop could tell these figures were women, and of course one was Sanrevelle. The pontoon man had just seen her.

With a new sense of mission, Hop paddled quickly toward the skiff, and as he got closer, there was something in the posture of the rear figure that reminded him of Sanrevelle, something eager and muscular. He could see the shape of a hoodie, too, so he stroked hard, his paddle clunking against the hollow aluminum, announcing his arrival. Now he was sure that it was Sanrevelle; he could almost see her smile, and as he drifted closer, only ten yards away, he saw what appeared to be a mound of neon treasure in their boat—rubies and emeralds and amethysts emitting a powerful glow.

"You want one?" a woman's voice asked. The voice came from the bow and was not Sanrevelle's.

Hop was now close enough to leap from his canoe to their skiff, but he couldn't make out their faces. The woman in the bow held out a piece of plastic jewelry, an oversize diamond ring lit from within. As he took it, the tip of his canoe touched the rim of their boat with a baritone clunk and the woman's face was briefly illuminated in gold. Hop saw that it was neither Sanrevelle nor Gwen.

"Thanks," Hop said, and put the ring on his fourth finger.

"Not a problem," she said, "but don't think this means we're married." Meanwhile, the figure steering

33

the outboard made no sound, her silhouette still opaque to Hop. "Sanrevelle?" he asked.

This rear woman said nothing, but the woman in front shook her head. "No Sanrevelle here," the first woman said. "Sanrevelle? Is that a name?" She didn't wait for an answer. "You stay safe out here, you hear? Keep that ring-light where people can see it."

And they puttered away, heading toward the assembly of glittering boats. By now the parade was a straight line, extending half a mile into the distance. Six boats away he could see a yacht with lights arranged in the shape of a jagged mouth. The penguin people had said Sanrevelle was there. The parade would pass right by him. All he had to do was wait.

"We can't wait!" Whistler had said the last time he'd seen him. Whistler was trying to get him to come to Florida with him, to a compound—at first Hop had heard *commune*—where they could do ayahuasca guided by experts in Further Father.

"Further father?" Hop had asked, and wondered if that was capitalized. Whistler had been discovering new terms, new theories, weekly, and this was another. Whistler's father had been dead for decades. Did this mean the founder of the fourth-largest personal-injury law firm on the West Coast missed his daddy? Could this happen to Hop, too? Would he turn fifty or sixty and suddenly need to be coddled, to make lists of childhood grievances, to be dazzled by theories because they almost rhymed?

On the other hand, there was this. There was water and light, there were oceans and holidays and sharks, there were people communing, there were boats and seals, there was Dean Martin, there was Jesus, there was now. Hop reached down and felt the cold water, brought some to his face and felt newly awake. A sailboat was approaching, its sails outlined in purple lights, its mast entwined in white. On the bow, a teenage ballerina was holding a swanlike pose, her hands using the halyards for balance. The next boat was a three-story pleasure cruiser, lights like icicles hanging from every level, and a solitary couple, an older man and woman, dressed as Santa and Mrs. Claus, sat high in the cockpit.

The shark-yacht was now approaching and a dread came over Hop. Did she want him to find her? After all, she'd told him she'd be at her boat and she had not been at her boat. She'd said that as a last resort she'd be at the Waterfront Social Club, and she hadn't been there, either. And she hadn't answered her phone. So the cues were clear. She was not looking to spend time with Hop this night or any night.

A foghorn sounded nearby, as if to punctuate this revelation. Hop stopped paddling and coasted for a moment, the heavy oily sea beneath him like the scaly back of a vast sleeping monster. He turned toward the shore, knowing he should go home. *Read the signals*, he told himself.

But he had a tendency to invent reasons to go forward, to ignore obvious discouragements and press on. When he was thirteen, old enough to know better, he'd decided he would be a hurdler. He'd seen Edwin Moses run, Edwin Moses with his receding hairline and goggle-glasses, looking so professorial and utterly out of place, and Hop had decided then that he would be a hurdler, too. He signed up for an open track meet at his school, pestered his mother to buy him spiked shoes, and at the day and time, Hop lined up with every other runner, mimicking their stretchings and other preparations. When the gun went off, he was fine, he pumped his legs and arms in a convincing way, until the first hurdle, which collapsed upon him like a bear trap. When he got up, he was bleeding from the nose and knees, but still he got up and attacked the second hurdle with fervor. This second hurdle caught his instep and threw him to the red clay, clavicle first, forehead second, and that was the end of his hurdling dream. No one clapped, no one told him "Nice try." He simply made his way back to his duffel bag, stuffed his shoes inside, and walked home barefoot.

This quest in the black water was no different. He would arrive at the shark-yacht, and Sanrevelle, if she was there at all, would be shocked, mortified, and would, at best, wave to him and tell him she'd see him another time, at their next lesson—some way of redrawing their boundaries. Nothing would be lost.

But then again, hadn't she given him occasional encouragement? During their last lesson, in the first week of December, it had hailed as they were coming in, but she still let him steer as she reefed the sails, let him steer the *Cradle* all the way into the marina. And afterward she'd invited him down below, to wait out the storm in her musty cabin, and they'd had tea, and she'd offered him a blanket, and she'd served him zucchini fritters. Surely she didn't do this for just any student.

"I'm actually going to the Sea of Cortez," she said. "Soon. January. So…" And then she'd looked at him for just a beat longer than she ever had before. Then she'd lowered her eyes, back to her tea. "It's open-ended. I might stay down there awhile. Just in case that matters."

In the moment, Hop hadn't read much into it—he'd assumed she was talking about a long pause in their lessons. But his Edwin Moses mind emerged in the days afterward, until finally he was convinced that she wanted him to come with her to the Sea of Cortez. And that she was leaving soon, and she might not be back anytime soon, so if he wanted to come, he'd damned well better make his intentions clear.

And what if she *did* take him? The thought of waking up on her boat, crawling up to the deck, seeing her at the helm, sailing into the sun— My god, he thought, could the world be ever be that good?

A splash behind him turned his head. He assumed it was a seal, but he found a man in a small aluminum boat. Hop hadn't heard him approach.

"Peter Pumpkin!" the man said. "What are you doing *now*, Peter Pumpkin?" The man was so close Hop could smell the medicinal stench of fermenting booze. He wasn't just passing by. He'd come to investigate. "Peter Pumpkin, you're not the one who's been poking around the *Sequoia*, are you? You can't go creeping around people's private boats, private homes, Peter Pumpkin. You know that, don't you? Are you smart enough to know that?"

"I'm not whoever you're looking for," Hop said. "I don't even know what the *Sequoia* is."

"We've seen a canoe like yours a couple times, and then afterward we keep finding certain things missing. You know anything about that, Peter Pumpkin?"

"I just borrowed this canoe tonight, from the Club."

"Okay, and maybe you borrowed it another time, too."

"No," Hop said. "You're wrong and I'm—"

"Shut it!" the man snapped. He took a few long breaths. "Okay, Peter Pumpkin. But I'm not the only

39

one watching what you're doing. And I'm not the only one willing to protect the *Sequoia* you say you don't know anything about. Just know that it'll be dangerous for whoever comes close again. Have a nice procession, Peter."

"Shut the fuck up," Hop said.

"What?" the man said.

Hop had no idea where his own words were coming from. "I said shut the fuck up or I'll drown you." The threat came from some volcanic place within him, and the man went still, his mouth open. Any menace he had presented to Hop was gone, but his skiff was still between Hop and the parade.

"I'm looking for Captain Sanrevelle," Hop said, "and I need you to get the fuck out of my way before I put this paddle through you."

Without a word, the man put his motor in reverse and his boat gurgled backward. "Jesus, man. Don't get so harsh." He seemed near tears. "She's my friend, too." A long silence stretched between them, and the man's face slowly grew bright under the lights of an approaching yacht. "I'm Tyler," he said. "I've known her twenty years."

"Hi Tyler," Hop said. "Sorry for what I said."

"She's right there, anyway," Tyler said, and pointed to the enormous boat passing before them. It wasn't the shark-boat. This one was far brighter than any before it, ten thousand bulbs in red and white and green, and soon it was above him, and there was no boundary between sky and water, day and night. All was kaleidoscopic color, and laughter and music echoed across the bay and against the far hills. And then he saw Sanrevelle. She was among a dozen people inside, everyone in gold and white, and was she wearing antlers? She was.

"See?" Tyler said.

Hop began to paddle, but the yacht she was on was moving briskly. In seconds it had passed them and was speeding away. Somehow Hop hadn't thought of this— the fact that the parade was moving too fast, that its boats had engines, that he couldn't possibly keep up.

"Fuck, whatever, I'll pull you," Tyler said. He was quickly in front of Hop's canoe, and threw him a line from the stern. Hop grabbed it and the man gunned his little outboard. They followed the vast casino-ship, its lights shimmering wildly in its frothing wake.

"You didn't have to get so harsh," Tyler said again as they gained on the yacht. Hop apologized once more, and as they approached the yacht's stern, Hop had to think of exactly what he'd do when they got close. Jump from the canoe?

"What're you gonna do when I get you close?" Tyler asked. His face was bathed in the yacht's white light now; he looked like a neon Jesus, so gaunt and exhausted, and yet willing to make one more attempt at majesty.

He was pulling Hop's canoe, and the canoe was bouncing madly in the bright wake, and Hop thought he would have to somehow crawl forward in his canoe, and then jump to the man's boat, and then make his way from stern to bow there, and finally, if they could get close enough, he'd jump from the skiff to the yacht... Good Christ.

But he could do it. He was still young enough to do it, and he felt a strange calm about doing it. The skiff in front of him was weaving in the wake, and his canoe was shuddering and swerving, but Hop felt a serenity in knowing without a doubt that he would make it across, dry and unharmed. He was about to explain the plan to the man but then Sanrevelle appeared. She was standing at the back of the yacht, on a low platform, bathed in red light.

"Ty? What're you doing? You okay?" Now she was kneeling, ready to grab a line offered by Tyler.

"I'm fine," Tyler yelled. "It's this guy who needs you." And he threw a thumb over his shoulder toward Hop, bouncing in the wake.

"Is that Hop?" she said, squinting, and her mouth broke open into a wide, crookedly confused grin. "What is happening back there?"

And then he knew she would come with him.

And then she did. After some pleasantries with Tyler, and after she bade goodbye to her hosts and retrieved her backpack, she climbed down onto Tyler's skiff and crawled from bow to stern, and then crawled into Hop's canoe, and they cut free of Tyler—at some point she lost her antlers—and Hop paddled backward, and the canoe drifted from the wake of the bright boat with its thousands of lights, and they floated quietly out of the channel. Soon the water was calm and the parade moved almost silently in the distance, a gorgeous pageant of irrational color in the darkest night.

"Show me that you're not wearing those weird shoes," she said.

He showed her.

"Good. How'd you know I was out here?" she asked. "You're not wearing a life jacket."

"I asked around," Hop said. "And you're not either."

"So weird," she said. "I had a dream you'd find me out here."

It was so quiet and so black. Her face was purple in the light of the ringed moon. She was grinning impishly, looking so young, so happy, so tired.

"I know a place we should go," she said. "You have another paddle?"

"I don't," he said.

"Well, you can take me this time," she said, and she arranged herself on the floor of the canoe, facing forward, and slowly, blessedly, she lowered her wild mane of hair into his lap. "I'll tell you where we're going, and when we get there I'll kiss you, okay?"

And so he let her guide him.

DAVE EGGERS is the author of many books, including *A Hologram for the King*, *Heroes of the Frontier*, *The Circle*, *The Every*, and *What Is the What*. He is a member of the American Academy of Arts and Letters.

NOTES & ACKNOWLEDGMENTS

The author would like to thank Heather Richard for her expertise and friendship over these many years. Thank you, too, to Ava and Julius. Thank you to Annie Dills for the just-right cover and to Sunra Thompson. Thank you to Jenny Minton Quigley, Edward P. Jones and the O. Henry team. Thank you to the *Best American* crew. Thank you to Caitlin Van Dusen and Amy Sumerton. Thank you to Amanda Uhle, Dan Weiss, and India Claudy. Thank you VV. And thank you to Gerald Maa and C.J. Bartunek at *The Georgia Review*.

Sanrevelle is the seventh story in *The Forgetters* series of mini-books. If all goes according to plan, these stand-alone stories will someday be part of a larger work. Exactly when this will happen, no one can be sure.

BOOKS IN THE FORGETTERS SERIES

THE MUSEUM OF RAIN

Oisín Mahoney is an American Army vet in his seventies who is asked to lead a group of young grand-nieces and grand-nephews on a walk through the hills of California's Central Coast. Their destination is a place called the Museum of Rain, which may or may not still exist. A testament to family, memory, and what we leave behind. *Also check out the audio version, narrated by Jeff Daniels.*

THE HONOR OF YOUR PRESENCE
Winner of a 2024 O. Henry Award

A homebody niece and her adventurous, almost-British uncle begin to attend parties to which they are not invited–an innocuous lark that becomes a very funny and lyrical referendum on why humans congregate and celebrate. Named a Distinguished Story in *The Best American Short Stories*.

THE COMEBACKER

In this comic, lyrical story, Lionel is a beat reporter covering the San Francisco Giants. When a new pitcher is brought up from the minor leagues, he shows Lionel a rare, even unprecedented, ability to see the beauty in the game he's paid to play.

The Keeper of the Ornaments

Cole lives alone, has no pets, and has grown accustomed to a home life of profound quiet (not to say tedium). When a raucous household moves into the apartment next door, Cole assumes he'll have to move. But his new neighbors, and their very odd cats, see him differently than he sees himself. A powerful meditation on forgiveness, grace, and the happiness of being called upon.

Where the Candles Are Kept

Two seemingly sullen California teenagers are sent to visit their uncle Oisín in rural Idaho one summer, and ponder their escape soon after they land. In this wry and suspenseful story, all three are forced to decide who and what they care about, and if they have any role in the saving of a life.

The Ocean Is Everyone's but It Is Not Yours

Aurora Mahoney runs one of three vaguely competitive whale-watching businesses on the Monterey coast. It's a life of great beauty, wonder and camaraderie, but after one of her fellow captains retires, a new, and decidedly different, sort of captain takes his place. What had been a simple and charmed life is clouded by a sinister, and yet aloof, new force on the waterfront. A page-turning examination of what makes a paradise, and how easily one human can destroy it.

Author proceeds from this book go to McSweeney's
Literary Arts Fund, helping to ensure the survival
of nonprofit independent publishing.

www.mcsweeneys.net

McSweeney's, founded in 1998, amplifies original voices
and pursues the most ambitious literary projects.

WE PUBLISH:

McSweeney's Quarterly Concern, a journal of new writing
The Believer magazine, featuring essays, interviews, and columns
Illustoria, an art and storytelling magazine for young readers
McSweeneys.net, a daily humor website.

An intrepid list of fiction, nonfiction, poetry, art and
uncategorizable books, including the Of the Diaspora
series—important works of twentieth-century
literature by Black American writers.